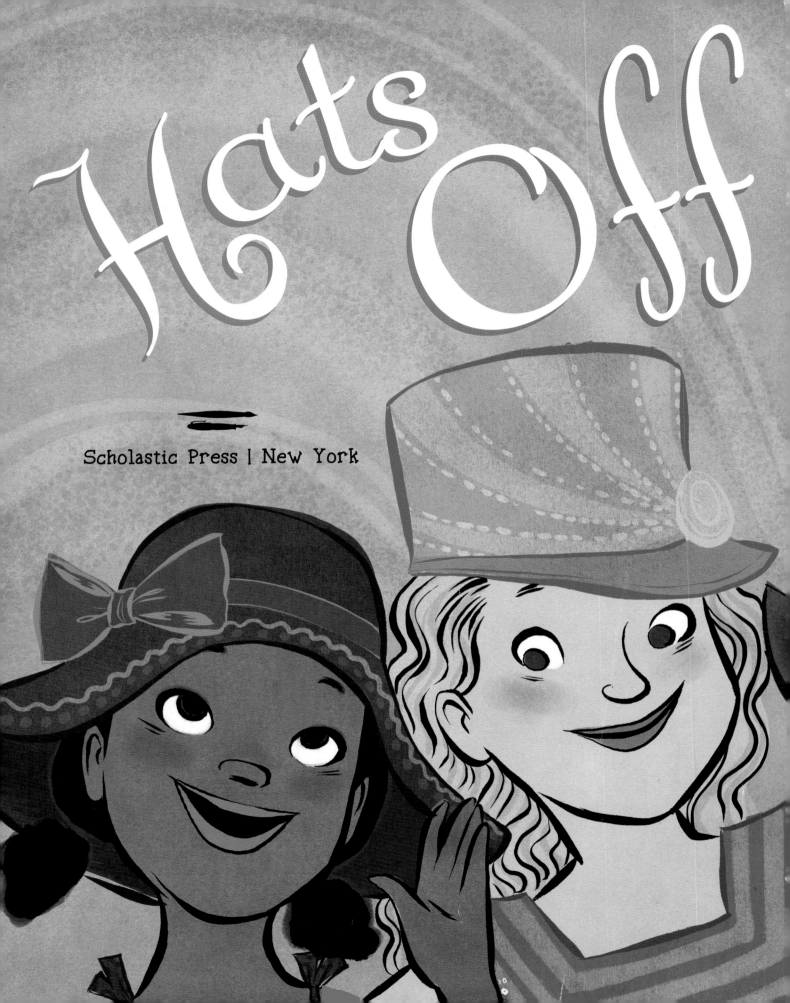

Hats Off

Scholastic Press | New York

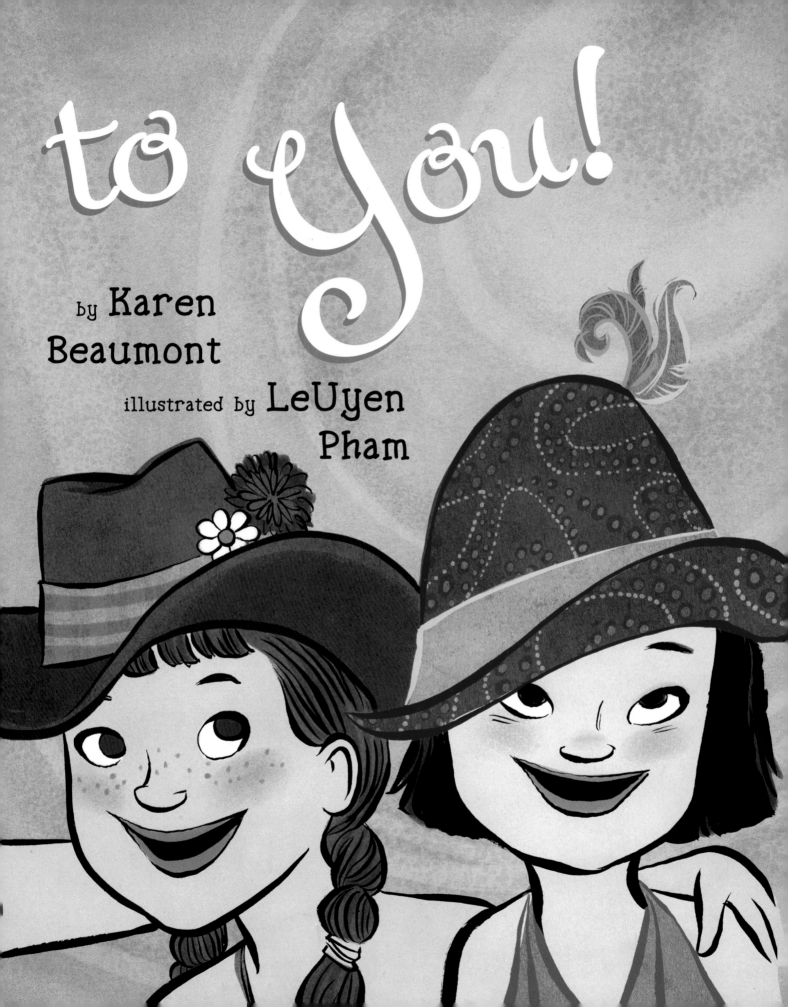

to You!

by **Karen Beaumont**

illustrated by **LeUyen Pham**

Emily, Ashley, Kaitlyn, Claire!
What is going on up there?
Sh-h-h! It's a secret we can't share.

We still need hats.
Come on, let's go!
The street fair's open
down below.

Chez Chapeaux! Look over there!
Hats are hanging everywhere.

Hats and more hats piled up high.
Which hats do we want to try?

Hats with flowers.

Hats with shells,

Hats with feathers,

Hats with bells.

Ribbons, buttons,
beads, and bows,

Gems and jewels . . . we all like those.

Hats with stripes,

And hats with stars.

That hat must have
come from Mars.

Big sombrero,

Cool beret—

We could try on hats all day.

Ooh-la-la! This hat's très chic.

Mine was made
in Mozambique.

Funky hat, to match my shoes.
I like girly curlicues.

Royal queen
    with sparkly crown.

I'm a silly
    circus clown.

Batter up!
    Eyes on the ball!

I just want to
    try them all.

Frou-Frou likes to
dress up, too.

No, no, Frou-Frou!
Don't you chew!

And now . . . our Hollywood debut . . .

Movie stars love fancy clothes.

Time for our red-carpet pose.

Emily, Ashley, Kaitlyn, Claire!

Need to
choose new hats
to wear.

Hats and more hats
piled up high.

Which hats
do we want
to buy?

Oh, my!

Pink or purple, red or white?
We think these will be just right.

One hat . . .
Two hats . . .
Three hats . . .
Four.

Tidy up, and
out the door.

Thank you, ma'am.
We love your store.

Emily, Ashley, Kaitlyn, Claire!
What is going on up there?

Still a secret we can't share.

All dressed up from head to toe.
Tiptoe down the stairs below.

One more thing to do. Let's go!

No fair peeking.
Close your eyes . . .

A mother-daughter tea!

Surprise!

We love our moms.
Hats off to you!
Thanks for everything you do.

Thank you, girls. We love you, too.

Hats off to YOU, Kim!
    Thank you for sharing your beautiful,
        loving heart with my girls.

                —K.B.

To Alize and Alora,
    my sweet little hat-loving nieces

                —L.P.

Library of Congress Cataloging-in-Publication Data available

ISBN 978-0-545-47423-8

10 9 8 7 6 5 4 3 2 1   17 18 19 20 21

Printed in China   62

First edition, March 2017

The art was inked with a Japanese brush pen and colored digitally.
The display font is based on Chikita Pro Regular.
The text type was set in Spellstone.
Art direction by Marijka Kostiw
Book design by Marijka Kostiw and Lillie Howard